PUNXSUTAWNEY PHYLLIS

by **Susanna Leonard Hill**

illustrated by **Jeffrey Ebbeler**

PUNXSUTAWNEY
PHIL

HOLIDAY HOUSE / NEW YORK

For Katie, Jon, and Hannah with love ~ Mom

For Eileen ~ J. E.

Text copyright © 2005 by Susanna Leonard Hill
Illustrations copyright © 2005 by Jeffrey Ebbeler
All Rights Reserved
Printed in the United States of America

The text type is Weidemann Bold.
The art for this book was done with acrylic paint
on oak veneer panels.

www.holidayhouse.com

3 5 7 9 10 8 6 4
Library of Congress Cataloging-in-Publication Data
Hill, Susanna Leonard.
Punxsutawney Phyllis / by Susanna Leonard Hill ; illustrated by Jeffrey Ebbeler.—1st ed.
p. cm.
Summary: Although she can predict the weather much better
than the boys in her family, no one thinks that Phyllis the groundhog
has a chance of replacing the aging Punxsutawney Phil
when Groundhog Day's official groundhog retires.
ISBN 0-8234-1872-3 (hardcover)
[1. Woodchuck—Fiction. 2. Groundhog Day—Fiction. 3. Sex role—Fiction.]
I: Ebbeler, Jeffrey, ill. II. Title.
PZ7.H55743Pu 2005
[E]—dc22
2003067641

ISBN-13: 978-0-8234-1872-5 (hardcover)
ISBN-13: 978-0-8234-2040-7 (paperback)

ISBN-10: 0-8234-1872-3 (hardcover)
ISBN-10: 0-8234-2040-x (paperback)

Phyllis was not like the other groundhogs.
She liked to get up in February instead of in March.
She liked to be outdoors instead of indoors.

When spring rains soaked the earth and
everyone else huddled in the burrow, Phyllis splashed
in puddles.

"You're sopping wet!" her mother scolded.

"I like the way the mud feels
between my toes," Phyllis explained.

Her mother shook her head and
said to Phyllis's father, "That's Phyllis!"

When the stream water rushed icy cold and fierce between the banks, Phyllis went wading. "You'll catch a cold," Aunt Patsy warned.

Phyllis's mother just shook her head. "That's Phyllis!"

When the August sun beat down, turning the meadow brown, Phyllis picked blackberries, warm and sweet. "You'll bake in this heat!" Aunt Sassy cried.

And guess what Phyllis's mother said?

"When I grow up," Phyllis said, "I'm going to be Punxsutawney Phil!"

"Don't be silly, dear," her mother said. "Punxsutawney Phil is a fellow!"

The other grown-ups laughed, but Phyllis knew she could do it, even if no one took her seriously.

And then, one February morning, Phyllis woke up early. She crawled out of bed and crept up the tunnel. The first light of morning shone at the mouth of the groundhog hole.

From the big pine trees came the steady *drip, drip, drip* of snow melting. Running water whispered in the brook. The air was sharp, but something about it had changed.

Spring was coming early!

She skipped back down the tunnel to wait for Uncle Phil to wake up and make his prediction.

"Phyllis, would you quit wiggling!" complained Phil Junior.

"Yeah, Phyllis," said Pete. "Some of us are trying to sleep."

"How can you sleep when spring is in the air?" asked Phyllis.

Phil Junior looked at Pete. "Only Phyllis would think spring was coming in the middle of winter!" he said.

"It's not the middle of winter," Phyllis said. "It's Groundhog Day."

But Phil Junior and Pete were already dozing off.

Pretty soon Aunt Sassy got up and tried to wake Uncle Phil. She shook him and tugged his whiskers. She shouted in his ear. Everyone else in the burrow woke up, but Uncle Phil kept right on snoring.

"What's all the ruckus?" asked old Grandfather Groundhog.

"It's Groundhog Day," said Aunt Sassy, "and Phil's still asleep! I'm afraid he's getting too old for the job."

"I'll do it!" Phyllis said eagerly. Everyone laughed.

"Punxsutawney Phil has never been a girl," said Pete.

"And never will be!" Phil Junior taunted.

"Nobody's going to get the job until Phil gives it up," said Aunt Sassy. "Now, how are we going to wake him?"

"Dump snow on him," Phyllis suggested.

"Good idea!" said Aunt Sassy.

It worked.

Uncle Phil grumbled.

"It's time to get up," said Aunt Sassy. "It's Groundhog Day."

"I'm sleepy," complained Uncle Phil.

"If you're too tired," said Phyllis, "I'd be happy to do the job for you."

"Harrumph," replied Uncle Phil. "Not just anyone can be Punxsutawney Phil!"

"I'm not just anyone," said Phyllis.

"Is your name Phil?" asked Uncle Phil.

"No," Phyllis admitted. "But Punxsutawney Phil's real name isn't always Phil."

"Yes, well," grumbled Uncle Phil. "But were you born on Groundhog Day?"

"I was born the day after," Phyllis said.

"Not good enough," said Uncle Phil. "Besides, you are a *girl*. When the time comes, one of those young fellows will fit the ticket!" Phil Junior and Pete smirked.

"They can't even feel that spring is in the air!" Phyllis said scornfully.

"We never have an early spring," said Uncle Phil. "In all my years as Punxsutawney Phil, it's never happened once."

"It's going to happen this year," Phyllis said stubbornly.

Aunt Patsy chuckled. "That's Phyllis," she said.

Phyllis wished people would stop saying that!

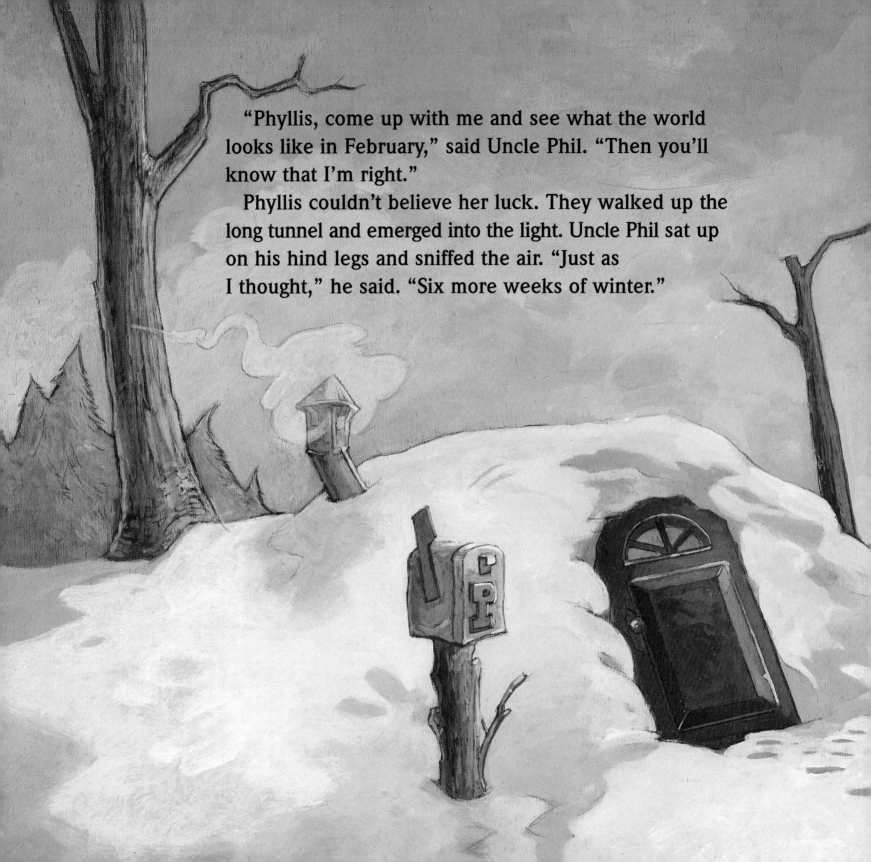

"Phyllis, come up with me and see what the world looks like in February," said Uncle Phil. "Then you'll know that I'm right."

Phyllis couldn't believe her luck. They walked up the long tunnel and emerged into the light. Uncle Phil sat up on his hind legs and sniffed the air. "Just as I thought," he said. "Six more weeks of winter."

"Early spring!" insisted Phyllis.

"Look at all that snow!" said Uncle Phil. "Feel the cold!"

"The snow is melting," said Phyllis. "The water is running in the brook."

Uncle Phil tilted his head and listened. "So it is," he said softly. "I don't hear as well as I used to."

"The chickadees are singing their spring song," said Phyllis.
"I've never heard the chickadees on Groundhog Day!" said Uncle Phil.
"And look, Uncle Phil. No shadows."
"My eyes aren't as clear as they used to be," said Uncle Phil.
"And don't you smell the sweetness of spring?" asked Phyllis.
Uncle Phil sniffed. "Just a hint," he murmured.

"And there's something else," said Phyllis. She had finally figured out what had felt different about the air all morning. "Feel the wind? It's from the west. The spring zephyr."

"Well I'll be jiggered!" said Uncle Phil.

"Phyllis was right," Uncle Phil announced when they returned to the burrow. "We *are* going to have an early spring. It's time for me to retire."

"But who will be the next Punxsutawney Phil?" asked Aunt Patsy.

"I will!" said Phil Junior.

"No, *I* will!" said Pete.

"Sorry, boys," said Uncle Phil. "You missed the signs too."

"You can't mean . . . ," blustered Phil Junior.

"Yes, boys," said Uncle Phil. "This time the best Phil for the job is a Phyllis."

"But what about the rules?" whined Phil Junior and Pete.

"If Mother Nature can bend the rules once in a while," said Uncle Phil, "we can too. Phyllis heard the water in the brook and the song of the birds. She saw that there was no shadow and she felt the spring zephyr."

"That's Phyllis!" her mother said proudly.

Phyllis grinned and said, "Punxsutawney Phyllis!"

WHAT IS GROUNDHOG DAY?

Groundhog Day is an American and Canadian tradition that is celebrated every year on February 2. Why February 2? Because that day is the midpoint of winter, falling exactly halfway between the winter solstice and the spring equinox. Groundhog Day has its roots in the European tradition of Candlemas Day, also celebrated on February 2. In medieval times, superstition held that if the weather on Candlemas Day was fair, the second half of winter would be cold and stormy, but if Candlemas Day was cloudy, the rest of winter would be mild and spring would come early.

According to an old English saying:

If Candlemas be fair and bright, Winter has another flight.
If Candlemas brings clouds and rain, Winter will not come again.

In Scotland, the saying was:

If Candlemas Day is bright and clear,
There'll be two winters in the year.

The Germans said:

For as the sun shines on Candlemas Day,
So far will the snow swirl until May.

If the sun shone on Candlemas Day, an animal would cast a shadow. Frightened, the animal would run back to its burrow, thus predicting six more weeks of winter. In Germany the animal weather predictor was a hedgehog. When German settlers came to Pennsylvania in the 1700s, they found no hedgehogs. But they did find groundhogs. Groundhogs, also known as woodchucks, are members of the marmot family and are actually a type of squirrel. They are small, furry animals, about the size of a large cat, that live in burrows in the ground and hibernate in winter. The German settlers decided that the groundhog, which resembled the European hedgehog, was a sensible, intelligent creature that would surely be wise enough to scurry back inside its burrow for six more weeks of winter if it saw its shadow on February 2.

WHO IS PUNXSUTAWNEY PHIL?

In Canada, the length of winter is predicted by a groundhog named Wiarton Willy. In America, that job belongs to Punxsutawney Phil. In the late 1800s, Clymer H. Freas, a newspaper editor, and W. Smith, an American congressman and newspaper publisher, organized and made popular a yearly festival in Punxsutawney, Pennsylvania. They chose a male groundhog to be the weather forecaster and named him "Punxsutawney Phil, Seer of Seers, Sage of Sages, Prognosticator of Prognosticators, and Weather Prophet Extraordinary." In his first performance on February 2, 1887, he saw no shadow and predicted an early spring.

In fact, Phil is only correct in his predictions 37–39 percent of the time, but don't tell him!